Rugrats

SIGHT for SORE EYES

by Luke David
illustrated by Barry Goldberg

SCHOLASTIC INC.

New York Toronto London Auckland Sydney
Mexico City New Delhi Hong Kong

KLASKY CSUPO INC.

Based on the TV series *Rugrats*® created by Klasky/Csupo Inc. and
Paul Germain as seen on Nickelodeon®

ISBN 0-439-11534-5

12 11 10 9 8 7 6 5 4 3 2 1   9/9 0 1 2 3 4/0

Printed in the U.S.A.   23

First Scholastic printing, September 1999

It was lunchtime, and Tommy sat in his high chair. He watched a spoonful of tiny carrot cubes glide toward him through the air. "Zoom, zoom!" his mom Didi crooned. "Coming in for a landing!"

Tommy shut his mouth tight and shook his head "No."
"C'mon, sweetie," pleaded Didi. "Carrots will help you grow
big and strong!"

"And what's more, they're good for your eyes," Didi waved the spoon. "Eating carrots will help Tommy see better!" She pushed the spoon toward him. Tommy swatted it. The tiny orange cubes cascaded to the floor. *Splat!*

The kitchen door slammed. Tommy's dad Stu led Spike in on a leash. "I'm so glad you're back, Stu," said Didi. "For the life of me, I can't get Tommy to eat his carrots. And you know how important Dr. Lipschitz says carrots are to the development of the individual!"

Klonk! Spike bumped into a chair.

Didi was alarmed. "My goodness! What did the vet do to Spike?"

"Not to worry. He just had some eyedrops," answered Stu. He patted the dog. "Old Spike will be fine soon. But for a while, I'm afraid our best friend is as blind as a bat."

Bonk! Spike bumped into the high chair and tumbled onto the floor.

Tommy bolted straight up in his chair.

Didi helped Spike to his bed and gave him a treat. "Oh, Stu, you left Spike's flea collar at the vet's!"

Dingdong! The doorbell rang. Stu scooped Tommy up, and they went into the living room to answer it.

Chuckie's dad had brought Tommy's friends Chuckie, Phil, and Lil over to play.

"Guys, something awful has happened!" said Tommy. "My dad left Spike's see-collar at the pet's, and Spike is a blind bat! We've got to get his eyesight and his whole self back to Norman!"

"Who's Norman?" asked Phil.

"But Tommy, we don't got a see-collar," said Chuckie. "Spike is doomed, doomed, doomed."

"We can't give up that easy, Chuckie. There must be another see-collar around here somewhere!" Tommy insisted. "When I run out of diapies or raisins, my mom can always find another package. Let's look. C'mon!"

"This is a good see-collar," said Phil. "But I think it's for a doggie who is more fatter than Spike."

"This see-collar is so bright and sparkly!" said Lil. "But I don't know why Tommy's mommy would keep such a prettyful thing locked in that big metal box!"

"Let's wake up Spike!" said Tommy. "Then we'll see if the sparkly see-collar works!"

Tommy shook his dog. Spike stood up and took a few steps.

Smack! Spike bumped into the TV.

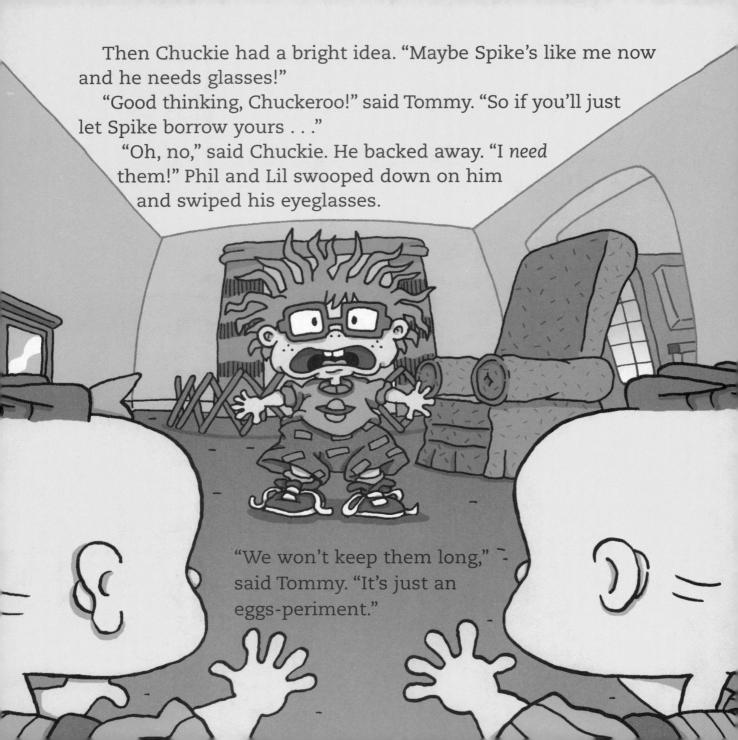

Then Chuckie had a bright idea. "Maybe Spike's like me now and he needs glasses!"

"Good thinking, Chuckeroo!" said Tommy. "So if you'll just let Spike borrow yours . . ."

"Oh, no," said Chuckie. He backed away. "I *need* them!" Phil and Lil swooped down on him and swiped his eyeglasses.

"We won't keep them long," said Tommy. "It's just an eggs-periment."

Thonk! Without his glasses Chuckie bumped into the easy chair.

Tommy put the eyeglasses on Spike.

Crash! Spike careened into the coffee table.

"Spike's eyes are getting worser and worser," said Tommy. "The eyeglasses don't work. The see-collars don't work. Nothing we've tried works. And I know why! My mom said my dad left the see-collar *at the pet's*. We got to get it from there!"

"But at whose pet's, Tommy?" whined Chuckie. "Spike is your only pet and he doesn't have one."

"I know. But what do we do when we got a problem we can't solve?" asked Tommy.

"Ask Susie!" shouted Phil and Lil.

"Right!" answered Tommy. "C'mon, everyone! Through the fence!"

"I don't have one solution to your problem," said Susie. "I have seven—seven pets!"

"That iguana is eating a bug," said Lil. "Goodie. Maybe he'll share."

"I wish I could hide in my shell like that turtle," said Chuckie, "because Tommy's mom will be real mad when she finds out we left the yard."

"Don't worry, Chuckie," said Tommy. "We'll go home now. Your pets are really nice, Susie, but their see-collars are all way too small for Spike. Thanks anyhow. Bye."

When the babies came home, Spike still couldn't see. "There's nothing for us to do now but nap," said Tommy.

Tommy dreamt about his lunch. The dream gave him an idea.

"Wake up, you guys. Wake up!" Tommy yelled. "I know how we can help get Spike back to Norman. Let's go!"

"Oh, boy, we're gonna meet Norman!" said Phil and Lil in one voice.

The babies went downstairs to the kitchen and found the carrots in the fridge.

"Those orange cubes look slimy," said Phil. "Yum! Yum!"

"Why do I always have to be on the bottom?" wailed Chuckie. "I can't see what you guys are doing!"

On his bed Spike snored and opened his mouth wide. Tommy shoved in a spoonful of carrots. Spike woke up, swallowed, and took a step. He walked across the kitchen without bumping into anything!

"Hip-Hip-Hurray!" cheered Tommy. "I say what's good enough for Spike is good enough for me!"

"Yeah, me too!" agreed Chuckie.

Phil and Lil chimed in together, "C'mon, let us have some too!"

Didi came into the kitchen and exclaimed, "Thank goodness! Spike's eyedrops have finally worn off and he can see again. Oh my, Stu! Look at the children. They're eating carrots. Now *that's* a sight for sore eyes!"